The Tragedy of Macbeth

Sweet Cherry
Publishing

Published by Sweet Cherry Publishing Limited
Unit E, Vulcan Business Complex,
Vulcan Road,
Leicester, LE5 3EB,
United Kingdom

First published in the USA in 2013
ISBN: 978-1-78226-078-3

©Macaw Books

Title: The Tragedy of Macbeth
North American Edition

Text & Illustration by Macaw Books 2013

www.sweetcherrypublishing.com

Printed and bound by Wai Man Book Binding (China) Ltd. Kowloon, H.K.

About *Shakespeare*

William Shakespeare, regarded as the greatest writer in the English language, was born in Stratford-upon-Avon in Warwickshire, England (around April 23, 1564). He was the third of eight children born to John and Mary Shakespeare.

Shakespeare was a poet, playwright, and dramatist. He is often known as England's national poet and the "Bard of Avon." Thirty-eight plays, 154 sonnets, two long narrative poems, and several other poems are attributed to him. Shakespeare's plays have been translated into every major existent language and are performed more often than those of any other playwright.

Macbeth: He is a Scottish general and the Thane of Glamis. Macbeth commits murder after murder once the prophecy of the three witches—that he would become the Thane of Cawdor—comes true. He is a brave soldier and powerful, but easily tempted.

Lady Macbeth: She is a deeply ambitious woman who will stop at nothing to have power and position. At the beginning of the story she is ruthless, but later she is driven to insanity and becomes victim to her guilt.

The Three Witches: These are three mysterious hags who plot mischief against Macbeth by using their spells and prophecies. Their prediction prompts Macbeth to commit murders.

Macduff: He is a Scottish nobleman who is hostile toward Macbeth's rule. He seeks revenge against him for murdering his wife and child.

The Tragedy of Macbeth

During the reign of the great King Duncan of Scotland, there lived a most able and gallant thane (lord) called Macbeth. Not only was

he close to the king, but he was
also his most able general during
war. He alone could vanquish
large and powerful armies,
driving them into a state of
complete disarray and panic.

Very recently, the reign
of King Duncan had faced
a threat from a rebel, the
Thane of Cawdor, assisted

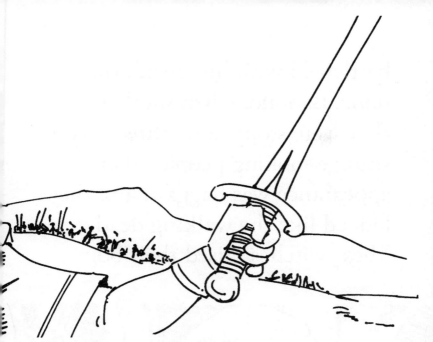

by the troops of their enemy,
the King of Norway. But
no threat could concern the
valiant Macbeth. Within a
few days, the thane army was
completely routed and the
Scottish Army was left victorious.

Now, the story of Macbeth
begins from the time of this
war. He was returning from the

battlefield with his friend, the
noble Banquo, when suddenly
they were stopped by three very
strange-looking people. Their
appearance was haggard and they
looked like the walking dead.
These witches raised their bony

fingers to their skinny lips and motioned the men to stop. Then the first one turned to them and said, "All hail Macbeth, the Thane of Glamis!" Macbeth was not surprised

to hear this, as he indeed was
the Thane of Glamis, and he
guessed these old creatures
must have recognized him.
But what came next shocked
both Macbeth and Banquo.

The second witch now
walked up to Macbeth and said,
"All hail Macbeth, the Thane of

Cawdor." And before Macbeth could react, the third witch came forth and exclaimed, "All hail Macbeth, he who shall be king hereafter!"

Now the three witches turned to Banquo and said, in turn, "Lesser than Macbeth, yet greater;" "Not so happy, yet much happier;" and "You shall beget kings, though you shall not be one."

Leaving the two men completely

dazed, the three witches
vanished into thin air.

Macbeth and Banquo once
again set off toward King
Duncan's palace, when they
were greeted on the road by
some of Duncan's soldiers.
After greeting one another, the

soldiers informed Macbeth that since the Thane of Cawdor had betrayed Duncan and led his armies against him, the king had declared that he would be hung. He also told the duo that Duncan had named Macbeth the new Thane of Cawdor as a reward

for his gallant and loyal services
to the throne over the years.

Macbeth and Banquo could
only gape at the messengers and
could not believe what they
were hearing. It had only been
a short while since the second

witch had told Macbeth he would be appointed the Thane of Cawdor! How could this be possible?

And so, Macbeth started wondering if the

witches could really have seen the future! They had said he would be the next Thane of Cawdor, which had come true, so perhaps they had also been right about the fact that he would be the king too! But then, Macbeth concluded that it could just have been a pure coincidence and therefore, there was nothing much to think about. He was of course elated at being appointed the

Thane of Cawdor and thanked
the messengers for bringing
him such delightful news.

That evening, when
Macbeth met Duncan, the great
King of Scotland, he invited him
to spend a day with him in his
castle. Duncan readily consented.

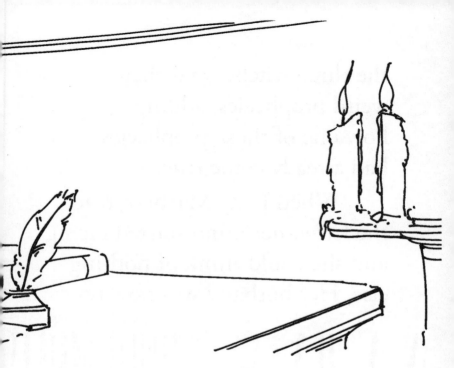

Now Macbeth needed to get
his castle in order for the king's
arrival. So he wrote a letter to his
wife, Lady Macbeth,
and told her about
the plan. While
writing, he
also mentioned

the three witches and their
weird prophecies, adding
how one of those prophecies
had already come true.

When Lady Macbeth read
the letter, her mind started racing
and she could think of nothing
else. Her husband was now no

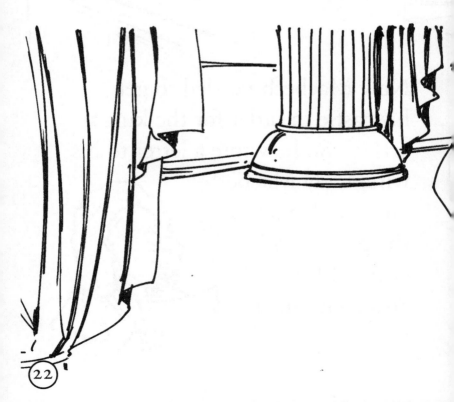

longer just the Thane of Glamis
but also the Thane of Cawdor, as
per the prophecy. Lady Macbeth
was therefore convinced that
her husband would soon be
the new King of Scotland.

Since Duncan was coming
to their castle that evening,
all they would have to do was

kill him and then the witches'
second prophecy would also
come true. If Macbeth was
destined to be king, Duncan
had to die that night.

When Macbeth
returned to his castle,
Lady Macbeth confided
in him about her

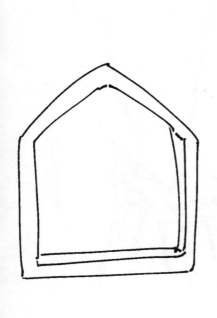

plans. At first Macbeth was completely against the idea of killing Duncan, because he felt that as his subject and his host, it was his duty to defend him and keep him safe. But Lady Macbeth refused to listen to reason, and finally managed to convince her husband.

That night, as Macbeth
waited for his wife's signal to
kill Duncan in his chambers, he
suddenly saw a dagger dangling

before him. At first
Macbeth assumed it was
a dream, and that if he
got up it would disappear.
But when he saw that
the vision of the dagger
kept following him, he
could not understand what
was happening to him. He
said to himself, "Is this a

dagger that I see before me, the handle toward my hand? Or are you a dagger of the mind, a false creation, proceeding from the heat-oppressed brain?" Unable to bear his infirmity any longer, at the sound of the bell tower chiming, Macbeth issued a warning. "The bell invites me. Hear it, Duncan, for it is a knell that summons you to heaven or to hell." So saying, Macbeth went to murder his own king.

Meanwhile, Lady Macbeth had arranged

to get Duncan's personal soldiers drunk and had placed the dagger next to Duncan for her husband to use. While she waited for Macbeth's return, she grew restless, scared that her husband might get caught in the act.

However, her mind was put to rest as soon as Macbeth returned with blood on his hands.

The couple soon retired to their rooms, where Macbeth washed off the blood and pretended to be asleep. Soon

it was morning and the king's
guards, Macduff and Ross,
arrived to rouse Duncan. But
all hell broke loose when they
realized that the king had been
murdered. They immediately
raised the alarm. Macbeth, on
hearing the news, appeared
to be enraged, and ran into

the room and killed the two
guards. The blame rested
on them, as they were killed
before they could deny their
involvement in the king's death.

Malcolm and Donalbain,
the king's sons, hurried out
of their rooms on hearing the
news. They realized that they

might be the next targets of the vicious murderer, so the two princes decided to run away from Scotland at once—Malcolm would flee to England, while Donalbain would rush to Ireland, where they would both be safe.

With the princes disappearing, some people began to wonder if they might be responsible for the death of their father. However, with the rightful heirs to the crown missing, Macbeth was anointed the new King of Scotland. The second prophecy of the witches had come true.

Macbeth at once settled into his new kingly duties. But he still had one thought nagging at the back of his mind—he was afraid that Banquo, his close friend of many

years, would suspect something was amiss. After all, Banquo was the only other witness to the witches' prophecies, and he might come to the conclusion that the murderer was none other than Macbeth. Therefore, he decided to have Banquo killed.

One night, Macbeth
arranged for a banquet for his
aides and ministers. Banquo,
along with his son, Fleance, was
supposed to attend, but alas,
Macbeth had other plans for
him. As Banquo set off, three
men came out of the bushes and
stabbed him. They tried to grab
Fleance as well, but Fleance's

horse, seeing the attackers
approach, galloped off into the
darkness and Fleance was saved.

But that evening, when the banquet began, Macbeth refused to sit down. When asked to join the others, he kept commenting on how the table was full. Though one chair had been left for him, Macbeth claimed he

did not see it, because in that chair sat Banquo's ghost. No one else could see the ghost and believed their king must be unwell. Macbeth, guilty

of the murder, kept saying, "You cannot say I did it. Do not shake your gory locks at me." Lady Macbeth, realizing that her husband was in a state of delirium, was scared that he might say more than he should. So she immediately told all those gathered

there that he was unwell
and asked them to leave.

Later, when Macbeth had
regained his sanity, he told
his wife that he would have to
pay the three witches another
visit, as he had to know what
else lay in store for him.

The next day, he retraced his steps along the same path he had taken the first time he met the witches. He found them boiling something in a large black pot behind a stone slab and asked them to tell him what his future would hold. The first witch started reciting something, after

which the face of an unknown
man appeared within the steam
coming from the pot. The
man told Macbeth, "Macbeth!
Macbeth! Macbeth!
Beware of Macduff!"
As soon as the
first image was
gone, another

face appeared, who said, "Be bloody, bold, and resolute; laugh to scorn the power of man, for none of woman born shall harm Macbeth." Macbeth was now very happy, because it was clear that the person who was going to kill him was not born yet. Finally, a third apparition appeared and informed him, "Macbeth shall never be vanquished until great Birnam Woods begin to walk against him." Again, Macbeth knew that this was not going to be possible, as trees couldn't possibly uproot themselves and start to walk.

However, Macbeth did not want to take any chances, so he sent some of his hired murderers to Macduff's castle. But Macduff had already left for England. On hearing that Macduff was not present, the murderers killed

everyone in the castle, including
Macduff's wife and child.

Meanwhile, Malcolm and
Macduff were in England, talking
about the affairs in Scotland.
Malcolm assured his friend that
the English royalty had been

very helpful and had provided
him with a battery of ten
thousand fine soldiers. He told
Macduff that there
would soon be an
attack on Scotland
to wrest the throne

away from Macbeth. While they were finalizing the plans, Ross arrived. He had just come back from Scotland and had some news. He told Macduff about the unfortunate event at his castle and the deaths of his wife and child. Macduff swore that he would return to Scotland and take his revenge against the perpetrator of this crime.

While plans to wage a war against Scotland were being discussed in England, a most queer thing was happening in the palace of the King of Scotland. The queen's maid had ordered

the doctor to come that night, as
there was a rather strange thing
happening that he needed to
see for himself. They waited for
quite some time after everyone
had gone to sleep. Then suddenly,
they heard a door open and
the light from a candle filled

the room. It was the queen. It
seemed that she was in some
sort of trance. She was trying to
scrub her hands and
kept saying, "Out,
out, damned
spot!" She kept
mumbling about

deaths and blood, and even mentioned Macduff's wife once. Finally, she exclaimed, "Will these hands ever be clean? They still smell of blood. Not even all the perfumes of Arabia can sweeten these hands!" Then, as mysteriously as she had arrived, she left.

The next day, the
whole of Scotland was
filled with the news
that the English Army
had arrived, led by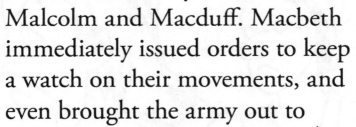
Malcolm and Macduff. Macbeth
immediately issued orders to keep
a watch on their movements, and
even brought the army out to

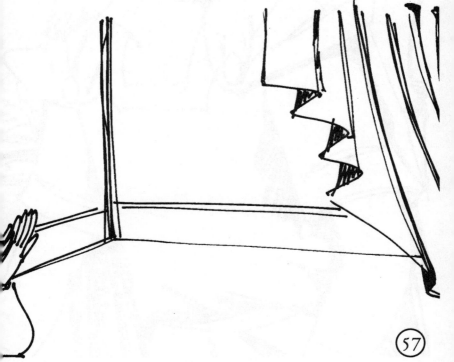

defend the castle at Dunsinane Hill in the event of an attack.

While the Scottish Army prepared to fight, the English Army camped at Birnam Woods. Malcolm instructed his men to break some branches off the trees and tie them to their bodies before laying siege to the castle. That way, their numbers would be misleading.

Macbeth was soon told by
a soldier that the woods were
approaching the castle. He
immediately remembered the
warning he had received from the
third apparition in the presence
of the three witches. He had
been warned that he would rule
until the great Birnam Woods
walked toward Dunsinane Hill.
As he was contemplating his
next course of action, a cry rang
through the palace walls. Lady

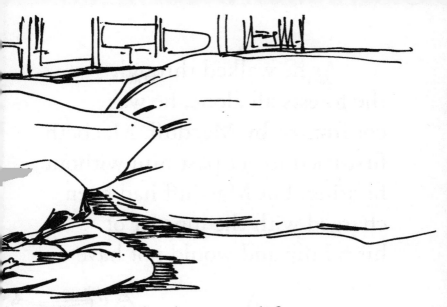

Macbeth had jumped from
the roof and killed herself.

Macbeth knew that his time
was also coming to an end, but
he was still comforted by what
the other apparition had
told him, that no man
born of a woman could
kill him. He decided
to put on his armor
and leave the castle.

As he walked through
the forests all alone, he was
confronted by Macduff. Macbeth
first tried to get past him without
fighting, but Macduff had been
charged with the murder of
his family and would not have

it any other way. Their swords clashed for a while, but neither man could gain any advantage.

Macbeth then claimed that no man born of a woman could kill him and that Macduff was wasting his time. To this,

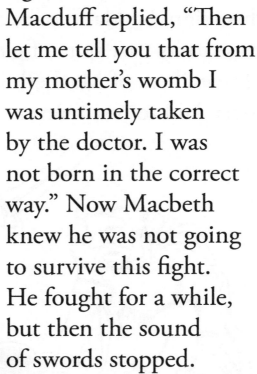

Macduff replied, "Then let me tell you that from my mother's womb I was untimely taken by the doctor. I was not born in the correct way." Now Macbeth knew he was not going to survive this fight. He fought for a while, but then the sound of swords stopped.

There lay Macbeth, at the feet of the valiant Macduff. All the prophecies had come true.

With Macbeth dead, Malcolm regained the throne that was rightfully his after the death of his father. Under his reign, Scotland once again rose to its past state of glory. The evil era of Macbeth had been laid to rest forever.